NOTHING LEFT TO LOSE

N.R. WALKER

COPYRIGHT

Cover Artist: N.R. Walker
Editor: Boho Editing
Publisher: BlueHeart Press
Nothing Left to Lose © 2024 N.R. Walker

Originally released as part of the 'Vegas, Baby!' Charity anthology in paperback format only.

ALL RIGHTS RESERVED:

This literary work may not be reproduced or transmitted in whole or in part in any form or by any means, including electronic or photographic reproduction, except in the case of brief quotations included in critical articles and reviews, without express written permission.

This literary work may not be reproduced or transmitted in whole or in part in any form or by any means, including information storage and retrieval systems, or for use in AI training software.

This is a work of fiction, and any resemblance to living or deceased persons, companies, events or places is purely coincidental. Licensed images are used for illustrative purposes only.

TRADEMARKS

All trademarks are the property of their respective owners.

BLURB:

When Brody Molina entered photos of him and Miller into a newlywed photo contest for a free weekend in Vegas, he didn't think they'd win. But they did. There's just one big problem: they're not actually married.

Miller Norton has been in love with his straight best friend forever. Tired of the heartache, he tries to put some distance between them. But then Brody wins a free weekend in Vegas. Against his better judgment—and as a last goodbye to their friendship—Miller agrees to play along.

It's a stupid, stupid idea, but hey, it's Vegas where anything goes. The stakes are high. But if Brody realizes he's ready to go all in, then Miller can roll the dice one more time, right? When there's nothing left to lose, maybe they'll both win.

N.R. WALKER

NOTHING LEFT to Lose

A LAS VEGAS SHORT STORY

CHAPTER ONE

MILLER NORTON

In the book of *The Most Stupidest Shit Miller Norton Has Ever Done*, this would have to be in the top spot.

It was a bad idea.

Like *bad* bad. And stupid.

This idea was so bad and stupid, it would be the crowning glory in the aforementioned book of the most stupidest shit I've ever done. It'd have its own chapter, for sure.

"Whatcha thinking about?"

Shit. I must've zoned out. "Huh?"

He pointed to my forehead. "You get a line right between your eyebrows when you're thinking."

I resisted sighing. He knew me too damned well.

"Uh, thinking that this is a bad idea."

Brody laughed, the kind of laugh where he threw his head back and got those cute little creases at the corners of his eyes.

See, therein lay the problem.

Brody Molina had been my best friend since our first year of high school. We'd been inseparable for eleven years, and I'd been desperately in love with him for every hopeless minute of those eleven years.

I had to wonder if he knew but he was too nice to let me down, and I was certainly too chickenshit to tell him.

Why?

Because he's straight, and I'm chickenshit.

We'd been through everything together. First heartbreaks, first kisses, first times, first jobs, first parties at college, first jobs.

Doing all kinds of stupid shit like skipping school at sixteen to get stoned and sneaking into the movies. Going to college classes still drunk from a party the night before, that kind of thing.

Other stupid shit too.

Like the first time he went all the way with Becky Kirsten and I had to pretend I was happy for him when, in reality, I'd gone home and cried myself to sleep.

When I came out as gay as a gangly fourteen-year-old, he was the first person I told. I braced myself for rejection. I even kinda hoped he'd hate me so I could learn to unlove him.

But nope.

He was awesome. He didn't care one bit. It changed nothing for him, he'd said.

But for me, it changed everything.

I loved him a whole lot more.

And so my years of teen angst and unrequited love morphed into my twenties of longing and heartache.

I was stupidly in love with my straight best friend.

And you might be thinking that this doesn't sound as if it deserves a whole chapter in my book of stupidest shit, but let me get to the good part.

Because we were sitting on a plane, taxiing towards the terminal in Las Vegas. Why are we flying from LA to Las Vegas for a three-day weekend?

Because my dearest best friend won an all-expense-paid weekend in a contest for newlyweds, that's why.

Yep.

Newlyweds.

That's where the stupidest shit comes into play.

Because the unrequited love of my life entered us into a contest to win the said fully paid-for trip to Vegas. He thought it'd be funny. He thought I needed a vacation. I'd been stressed lately, he'd said.

And yeah, that was true.

See, we had some photos taken at my sister's wedding. Of Brody and me in our suits, looking all kinds of handsome.

Looking all kinds of coupley.

Looking all kinds of newly married in the church, and then when we danced at the reception.

We always looked like a couple.

People always assumed we were a couple.

But nope.

Brody was straight.

The fact he'd hold my hand, or hold a door open for me, or stand closer than he probably ever needed to, didn't help.

Most of my potential hookups took one look at the way Brody was with me and assumed I was taken. I mean, he'd come to gay bars with me so I wouldn't have to go alone . . .

It certainly didn't help me and my hopeless heart.

So yes, this was stupid.

Because now we had to act like a newly married couple. Just for three days, and just in front of the hotel promo people and contest organizers. The rest of our time would be free for us to do whatever we wanted. And there was a gay pool party I was interested in.

But anyway, it had disaster written all over it.

Brody thought it was hilarious. And he thought I'd have no problem with it. And normally I might not have. To be fair, we acted like a married couple most of the time.

But I'd been struggling with it lately. Every time he'd smile at me, or laugh, or put his arm around me, or take my hand . . .

My heart ached.

And I was tired.

Tired of pretending it didn't hurt.

Pretending I didn't want to have what we had . . . but for real. I wanted him to look at me and know. I wanted him to lean in and press his lips to mine. I wanted him to love me like I loved him.

So yes.

Pretending we were married for the sake of a free vacation in Vegas was a stupid idea.

Stupid, stupid, stupid.

There was no way this was going to end well.

CHAPTER TWO

BRODY MOLINA

Miller needed this time away.

He'd been so stressed lately. Quiet and not himself. His smile didn't quite sit right, and his laughter fell flat.

That spark of light in his eyes that I'd always noticed was gone.

He'd said his job was a lot to deal with right now, and he'd been putting in some long hours. The last few times I'd suggested dinner or grabbing a few drinks, he'd been stuck at work. And then there was the whole stress of Paisley's wedding.

And, the truth was, I'd missed him.

He was my wingman. The Robin to my Batman. I couldn't remember a time in my life when it wasn't us against the world.

But lately, things had been different.

Something didn't feel right with him, and it scared me in ways I wasn't ready to unpack just yet. So I knew I *had* to enter us when I saw that newlywed photo contest with a fully funded three-day weekend in Vegas.

Plus, we'd gone to Paisley's wedding two weeks before and had those really cool photos of us, with the one near the altar in the church, which could totally pass as *our* wedding. And the dancing photo as well. We were slow dancing, and it just so happened to be a photo where Paisley in her wedding gown wasn't in the background, so it looed like *our* wedding dance . . .

Which it wasn't.

But still . . .

The photo looked like it was, and that was all we needed.

Literally.

"I can't believe we're doing this," Miller mumbled as we waited to check into the hotel.

"It'll be fun," I tried, giving him a nudge. "Free room and free booze for three days. It's gonna be great."

"No, I mean, I can't believe all it took was a photo to enter us. No marriage certificate or anything."

"It was a photo contest."

He made a face. "We're going to get found out."

"Stop stressing. All we gotta do is look all coupley. Be all cutesy with the sexy gay vibe. You know they love that shit."

Miller's gaze shot to mine, hard and fierce, and I knew I'd said the wrong thing. "That shit?"

Goddammit.

"You know what I mean. The sexy gay couples all

over Instagram and TikTok. They want the photo ops and—"

"That *gay shit* isn't something I can turn on and off for a photo op, Brody. Jesus Christ."

I put my hand on his back, sliding it down and pulling him closer than was probably necessary and giving him my sad puppy face. "I didn't mean it like that. I'm sorry."

Did I know that he'd forgive me for anything when I did that? Maybe.

Was that why I did it?

Yes.

I had absolutely zero problem with being handsy with Miller. We'd always been that way. It was why people often assumed we were a couple, because we were always handsy. Okay, correction. I was handsy with him. He was never handsy with me, but he was totally okay with me putting my arms around him, taking his arm or his hand, dancing with him.

So me putting my hand on his lower back and pulling him against me was nothing. Me pouting and batting my eyelashes until he smiled was par for the course.

But damn, for a minute I thought it wasn't gonna work. He was really mad at me. But then the corner of his lip began to curl up and he rolled his eyes. "You're such a jerk," he mumbled.

"Can I help you?" the lady behind the counter said.

Oh, it was finally our turn. I dropped my arm from

Miller's back and stepped up to the desk. "Ah, yes. We have a reservation. Brody Molina and Miller Norton."

She tapped her keyboard and stared at the screen for a second before giving us a blinding smile. "Oh, yes, the newlywed contest winners! How wonderful."

Oh boy.

Here we go.

"Yes, that's us," I said.

No going back now.

We confirmed our booking and a few moments later were presented with our room keys. "The honeymoon suite," she proclaimed proudly. Smugly, almost, as she slid the key cards toward us.

Like she presumed we'd be having all kinds of newlywed sex in that honeymoon suite.

Like most people would expect newlyweds to do . . .

Gawd.

Before I could lose my nerve, before I could agree that this was a very bad idea, I took the keys and played along with the lie. "Thank you," I said cheerfully.

I turned to Miller with the intent of getting to the room ASAP when the reception woman offered me a printed piece of paper. "And here's your itinerary."

Itinerary?

I scanned the letter, horrified to see it was basically a full list.

"Carina left a message to say welcome and that she'd see you at four o'clock."

Carina was the contest lady who I'd dealt with.

Who I'd lied to.

And sure enough, there on the itinerary at four o'clock was *meet and greet with Carina in hotel lobby.*

Which meant we had about an hour.

We bundled into the elevator, Miller's eyes meeting mine in the mirrored wall. He didn't say anything but half-rolled his eyes and shook his head when someone else walked in. We rode in silence, and when we walked into our suite, he stopped dead and dropped his duffle bag at his feet.

We stood there a moment in silence, both of us staring at the huge bed.

The *one* bed.

One huge, soft, and comfy-looking, expensive-looking bed.

With a heart of rose petals on the duvet, and a bottle of Moët on ice.

Ohhhh boy.

"The bed's plenty big enough for both of us," I tried. We'd shared a bed before. This was no big deal.

Miller took the bottle of champagne, unwrapped the gold foil, looked me dead in the eye, uncorked it like a pro in one smooth pop, then began to chug it straight from the bottle.

Right then.

He made a face as he stopped for air. "So tell me, what's the felony charge, exactly, for the crime we're committing? Just trying to do the math on that. Like, will I be out of prison for my thirtieth? Because Mom was already talking about my grandparents visiting from Florida."

"There won't be any felony charges," I said.

I think . . .

"And anyway, your thirtieth is like five years away. She's planning it already?"

"You know what she's like." He chugged more Moët while we both seemed stuck staring at the bed.

"And I still can't believe your grandparents moved to Florida. I loved their house in the hills."

Miller nodded and handed me the bottle of champagne. "Same."

I took a decent mouthful, and then another.

Miller let his head fall back with a groan. "We are *not* gonna be able to pull this off."

I gulped the Moët and swallowed down the belch that threatened to escape. "Sure we will. There's nothing we don't know about each other. What can they ask us that we don't know?"

"It's not the trivia I'm concerned about."

No. He meant the physical stuff.

"We'll be fine," I said. "I'll be fine with it."

Miller replied with one raised eyebrow.

"What?" I countered. "I can pretend to be your husband, no problem." I put the bottle in the ice bucket and threw my arms around him to prove my point. I rested my chin on his shoulder. "You know I'll be fine with it."

He . . . didn't react. Didn't lean into me like he typically did, didn't turn around and hug me back. Didn't laugh or joke about it. He didn't say a word.

He did nothing.

It was almost as if *he* had a problem with it.

But he was gay. He never had a problem with a guy hanging off him. Lord knew I'd seen guys fawn all over him before and that was fine . . . kind of. I mean, *he* was fine with it.

It was almost like the problem he had here was me.

Wait.

I froze as realization dawned. "Miller," I said, turning him around so I could see his face. "Do you not want to do this?"

"It'd be too late now if I did, wouldn't it?"

"Mills," I tried. That nickname normally softened him like butter, but not today. He tried to look away, so I put my hands on his face to make him look at me. Something really wasn't right with him. "Are you okay?"

"I'm fine."

He wasn't, clearly.

He pulled his face from my hands but he didn't move away, so I pulled him in for a fierce hug. I don't know why hugging him always made me feel better, but it did. It gave me peace, and I hoped it did the same for him. "We'll be okay," I murmured. "It's just one weekend. We'll be fine. We'll have a few drinks, relax, and have a great time."

There.

That was good. Reassure him that it was just me and him, like the old days, and that I wanted to make this about him. For him to have a great weekend, relaxing and maybe feeling like his old self.

He sighed and pulled away from me. He threw his bag on the bed. "You're on the left side."

"As always."

He took the Moët bottle and guzzled more of it, squinting as he swallowed. He looked at the remaining contents, then at me. "We're gonna need a fuckton more of this."

CHAPTER THREE

MILLER

So if we were doing this, I would be doing it drunk.

There was no other way I could get through it. Certainly not freaking sober. Social lubrication be damned. This was a pain buffer in the form of sparkling anesthetic, a hundred bucks a bottle.

One bottle of Moët later and I was feeling marginally better. Well . . . that wasn't exactly true. I still felt bad, but I cared a whole lot less.

Which was probably just as well, because we had to meet with the contest organizer.

I was letting Brody take the lead on that.

This was all his idea, after all.

"Ah, Brody and Miller," a woman greeted us. She was tall and thin, wearing a radio station T-shirt and a wide, bright lipstick smile. She shook Brody's hand first. "I'm Carina. Nice to meet you," she said, then she turned to me. "And you must be Miller."

I shook her hand with an easy Moët smile. I really should drink more Champagne. Not that I drank much of anything, but that warm, easy feeling was nice.

"That's me," I replied.

She asked about our flight and if we were ready for a great weekend, if we were excited.

Uh, no. I'm dreading it. And I'm drunk, so there's that.

"And how's married life treating you?" she asked with a squinty smile.

"Well," I began, because she was looking directly at me.

"It's great," Brody interjected. "So far," he added with a laugh. "It's all kinda new."

"So new," I said, a little drunker than I was just a minute ago. "So new it doesn't even feel real."

Brody put his arm around my shoulder, squeezing a little harder than necessary. "Incredible, huh?"

"Well, you were a clear fan favorite," Carina said. "Your photos were so beautiful."

"Yes, they were," I said, meaning every word.

I felt Brody's eyes on me but didn't dare look at him. Maybe he'd see through me, see it in my eyes that I almost cried when I first saw that photo of us dancing at my sister's wedding. How we were standing so close, our arms around each other, the way I was smiling at him.

God, I'd seen that photo and it broke my heart.

Because he'd never love me the way I loved him. And had loved him for almost half my life.

"Speaking of photos," Carina said. "Can we pose for a few?"

"Sure," Brody said.

A man with a camera appeared from nowhere, springing up with the radio station standee, and Brody and I were corralled next to it with the hotel name behind us. Promo, promo, promo. Whatever. If there was more Moët, I didn't care at all.

"Okay, face me," the photographer said. He waved us in. "Stand closer."

I slid my arm around Brody's waist and his arm went around my shoulder. We'd done this a million times. This was no different from any other photo we'd taken over the years.

No big deal.

"Okay, re-create the dancing photo," the guy said.

Dread and butterflies fought for airspace in my belly.

But Brody slid his hand down to my lower back and pulled me in close, far too naturally, far too comfortably. I pressed against him, allowing myself to have this just one more time.

A stupid photo op, nothing more...

He took my hand like we were ballroom dancing and we did a few slow steps, but it was ridiculous and stupid, and I laughed.

"Perfect," the photographer said.

I snorted.

"Okay, now kiss."

Aaaaand now I wasn't laughing.

Brody's eyes met mine. Fear and *what the fuck* stared back at me, and I almost faltered. I almost gave us away right then and there.

But then his gaze dropped to my lips and drew back up to my eyes, and something else stared back at me.

Determination?

Daring?

Then he slid his hand along my jaw, lifted my face, and pressed his lips to mine.

Soft and sweet and everything I'd ever wanted.

Everything I'd longed for, dreamed of.

My whole chest was aching and thrumming all at once. I pressed my forehead to his, my eyes closed—too afraid to look at him—trying to convince my heart that this wasn't real but to savor this moment anyway.

And not to break into a million pieces.

"Perfect," the photographer said, snapping me out of Brody's spell.

Looking at them, the photographer reviewed his camera screen and Carina smiled at us.

"Awww, so perfect," she crooned.

I dropped my hand from Brody's waist and took a step away, suddenly feeling a little lightheaded.

Brody grabbed my arm, then slid his hand down into mine, threading our fingers. "He cracked the Champagne in our room," he announced, as if that explained why I was suddenly dizzy.

As if it had nothing to do with the fact that Brody had just kissed me.

"He doesn't normally drink too much," Brody added, like it'd help.

I looked right at Carina. "Uh, yeah. That Moët is good. Any chances of another bottle?"

She found that cute, apparently. "I'll have a word with the hotel and see what I can do."

Brody squeezed my hand. "You'll need a nap if you have any more."

"Oh no," I joked. "A nap. How terrible."

Brody laughed, but he never let go of my hand. He was taking this *way* better than I was. Considering this was the first time he'd ever kissed a guy. That I knew of, anyway.

Christ.

What if it wasn't?

No.

No, I had to *not* think of that. He'd been with a stack of women before, and it never bothered me too much. But the idea of him kissing a man? A man that wasn't me?

The Champagne was threatening to reappear. The way my stomach turned . . .

He was completely unfazed, and I was spiraling. And I was the gay guy who'd had my share of men, kissing random strangers in clubs who'd meant nothing at all. Exactly how he'd just kissed me.

It was all a very blunt reminder. Proof that kissing me meant nothing to him.

"Miller?" Brody murmured, his eyes full of concern.

"Yeah, maybe a nap isn't a bad idea," I said. I grimaced at Carina. "Sorry."

She chuckled. "It's okay. Hope you're feeling better before dinner tonight."

Dinner?

We had to attend a dinner?

Jesus.

"See you there," Brody said as he waved her off and led me back to the elevator. He leaned me against the wall and his eyes met mine, clearly concerned. "That Moët really hit you hard, didn't it?"

It wasn't like I could tell him this was me freaking out, not me drunk.

Whatever.

"Mm. I think I need that nap."

In our suite, I made a beeline for the bed and fell onto it, lying on my back and pulling the pillow over my face. Brody lifted one of my feet and pulled my shoe off, then the other, and I hated that he looked after me like that.

The bed dipped, and I didn't need to look to know he was sitting beside me. "You okay under there?" he asked, his voice soft and sweet. I hated that he spoke to me like that too.

Everything he did messed with my head. He was one hundred percent boyfriend material. The perfect boyfriend for me. He was caring, sweet, supportive, funny, gorgeous ...

And straight.

And one hundred percent not my boyfriend.

Certainly not my husband.

"This is going to end so badly," I mumbled.

"It'll be fine," he replied.

I wasn't talking about the likely legality of it all. I was talking about us.

Not that I would tell him that.

"We did okay back there, right?" he asked. He sounded so insecure; it made me pull the pillow away so I could see his face. He looked as uncertain as I'd ever seen him. He was normally confident in everything he ever did. "I mean, the kiss." He grimaced. "Was it okay? I think we did okay. Without practice or without warning, or anything, really. I mean, we talked about it, but actually doing it was okay, right?"

Seeing him so unsure hurt me physically. I sat up and nudged him with my shoulder. "Are you okay with it?" I asked. Then, because I liked to inflict more pain on myself, I added, "I might even think it wasn't the first time you've kissed a guy before."

He laughed, his cheeks pink, and he ducked his head. "Well, yeah, of course it was."

Lord, his cute reaction almost did me in.

"Well, you fooled them both."

His eyes met mine. "I think it was the forehead thing you did that convinced them."

"The forehead thing?"

"Yeah, when you pressed your forehead to mine. Like you did in the photo."

Oh god.

Yeah, that was me trying to savor every moment and not expire at the same time.

I fell back on the bed and put the pillow back over my face. "One of my many moves," I joked. "It's called The Forehead Thing. Works every time."

Brody was quiet for a moment, and that sleepy, heavy feeling was settling over me. That nap was starting to sound really good. I patted the bed on the other side of me. "Nap time."

Brody climbed over me and lay down beside me, his arm resting heavily across my belly. "Thought you'd never ask."

"Since when do you ever wait for me to ask?"

"Well, now that we're married, I thought I'd try it."

I gave him a shove, and he laughed, but never moved his arm. I pulled the pillow off my face and shoved it under my head, but I kept my eyes shut.

Pretty sure he was looking at me.

Damn sure I didn't have the guts to look at him.

That stupid voice in my head told me to enjoy the moment. Enjoy the feel of his arm on me, enjoy the feel of him beside me in bed, because it was all I'd ever get.

After this weekend, I was sure of that.

The wheels would fall off at some point.

They had to.

Because my heart was nearing the finish line. I had to make a clean break and move on with my life and my unrequited love and get over Brody Molina, once and for all. This weekend would be the end.

Enjoy it while it lasts.

No, it's not real. It's all fake for some contest and a free weekend in Vegas. But all that shit in your head that you dreamed up over the years wasn't real either, so what the hell.

Enjoy this as a last hurrah, a fond farewell, a last goodbye.

Sure.

I'll consider myself the conductor of the band that played on while the Titanic sank.

Like he was a mind reader, Brody pulled me into his arms and held me. "You okay? You're mumbling to yourself again," he said.

I was going to protest but he felt so good against me. He smelled incredible and his arms were strong, his chest warm against my cheek.

So yeah, I could give myself one last weekend.

And the band on the Titanic continued to play.

CHAPTER FOUR

BRODY

Something changed in Miller when we woke up from our nap. Thank god I'd set my alarm, otherwise we'd have slept right through the stupid dinner thing. And it certainly didn't help matters when we woke up very pressed together.

I had no problem with intimacy with him. We'd always been close—the touchy-feely kind of best friends. It's just who we were. I hugged him all the time. I'd shared a bed with him before, dozens of times.

Never woke up with my leg over him and a raging hard-on though.

That was new.

Maybe my dick sent the wrong messages to my brain, looking for any kind of action. It'd been a while for me, and Miller was a warm body . . .

A warm body with a six-pack and hard muscles and sharp angles.

No softness, no breasts, no floral body sprays, no siree.

He was . . . definitely a man.

And I could appreciate a man's body. I knew when a guy was hot, when he was looking fine.

But I'd never been *attracted* to a man before. Except Miller, these last few months when it felt like he'd been avoiding me and I'd missed him like crazy. Wanted to touch him, imagined touching him, pulling him against me and hugging him like we used to do. Feeling him against me.

I'd never wanted to explore that with just *any* guy. Miller, sure. But that was normal, right? I'd never once wanted to take a dude home. But the idea of pressing up against Miller in bed right now, gripping his hip, and sinking my cock into his warm, tight heat. . . .

I shot out of that bed so fast, I almost gave myself an erection injury.

Because what the fuck?

It took a second for me to catch my breath.

My dick was just sending mixed signals, nothing else.

Warm body, too long since I'd had sex, nothing more.

I avoided all eye contact in the bathroom mirror and had the coldest shower I could stand.

It took care of my not-so-small problem anyway.

Until Miller walked in, still half asleep, scratching his head. "I need to piss," he mumbled. He didn't look at me being very naked in the shower. He just stood at the toilet, relieved himself, then washed his hands.

And never once did he look at me.

Now, we'd shared bathrooms before, no big deal, and I was pretty sure he'd never looked at me any of those times either.

So why did it bother me so much that he didn't look at me this time?

"Hurry up or we'll be late. I need to get in after you," he said as he walked out.

And for some deluded, fucked-up reason, I almost told him to join me.

And my dick was totally on board with that.

What—and not for the first time today—the ever-loving fuck?

I shut off the hot water and stood under the cold water until my dick behaved.

Christ.

When my teeth chattered, I got out and dried off as quick as I could. I wrapped the towel around me, extra tight, and held my dirty clothes in front of my traitorous dick as I walked out.

"Shower's all yours," I said, not making eye contact.

He disappeared, thankfully, and I busied myself getting dressed and ready, all while trying really hard not to think about Miller being naked and wet in the freaking shower.

The hell is wrong with my brain right now?
This was absurd.

I'd definitely have to jerk off tonight when he was asleep.

Yep, that'll fix it.

I just hadn't taken part in any self-care for too long apparently.

If one could consider yesterday morning in the shower before I picked him up for our trip as *too long*.

It was most definitely too long.

Think bad thoughts. Think terrible thoughts. Think disgustingly gross thoughts.

A knock at the door scared the shit out of me and I rushed to open it. It was a hotel staff member, dressed in their fancy uniforms. She was cute. Very much my type: long hair, big boobs, bright smile...

But not at all what I wanted.

What I wanted was in the shower right now.

God fucking dammit.

She was also holding another bottle of Moët and she offered to me. "As requested," she said. "Courtesy of—"

Miller chose that exact freaking moment to walk out of the shower, wearing nothing but a towel around his waist. His hair was wet and combed back, water beads across his chest.

"Oh," he said, balking. "I didn't know we had company, sorry."

I was still looking at his happy trail and the outline of his dick in that wrapped-tight towel.

I was losing my damn mind.

I turned back to the staff, who was also staring at Miller, eyes wide and clearly liking what she saw.

I took the bottle from her. "I'm gonna need this, thank you," I managed to say.

At this rate, I was going to need an entire cellar of it.

I tipped her, closed the door and leaned against it, trying to get a grip. But Miller was still standing there, still wet and almost naked... the towel didn't hide much.

"You good?" he asked, eyeing the bottle in my hands.

Then he turned around to grab his bag, and his ass in that too-tight towel was pure fucking art.

"Oh yeah, I'm fine," I squeaked.

I was absolutely not fine.

I was having impure thoughts about my best friend.

Who was a man, I needed to remind myself.

Yep.

My dick didn't seem to care.

And before I could do something completely inappropriate and mind-boggling, like walk over and push him onto the bed, I began undoing the champagne, quickly popping the cork and taking a long drink straight from the bottle.

"You ready to be husbands again?" he asked. "Ready to kiss me if you have to?"

I almost swallowed my tongue but was drunk enough that I smiled instead. "If I have to."

"Not weirded out?" he murmured.

"Not at all," I replied.

Absolutely not at all weirded out that I keep thinking about his body, his dick in that towel, the way he'd felt asleep next to me, what it felt like to kiss him before . . .

"I need food," I managed to say.

"Then let's get through this awful dinner and then we can hit the town."

"Hit the town? Who the fuck says that anymore?"

"I do. I just did. Stop being a dick and let's go eat."

Dinner was a great idea because food would help soak up the bottle of champagne we'd just demolished.

I'd drunk most of the second bottle and had a decent buzz on when we left to meet Carina again in the lobby.

Why we were meeting her in the lobby instead of the restaurant was something I probably should have clued into before, but the Moët-fueled buzz took the edge off all reasoning.

I was still too hung up on my newfound attraction to Miller to be thinking straight anyway.

Straight . . .

I snorted, and Miller shot me a look just before he hit the button on the elevator. "You okay?"

"Super," I lied, just as he slid his hand into mine.

I'd held his hand a thousand times before. This was no different. Except it was.

Somehow.

Because he held my hand first.

Had he ever been the one to take my hand first?

I wasn't sure . . .

I also wasn't sure why I *knew* that he'd never initiated contact.

It was always me.

Except before we came down, he'd fixed my shirt collar and then my hair. And then he'd gently tapped my chin with his finger and it did some weird buckling thing to my knees.

And my heart.

But I was ignoring that.

Like I was trying to ignore how he was different after our nap. He was the one who touched me first; he was the one being flirty. Not me.

Had he felt my hard-on when we were cuddling? Did he misread that for something it wasn't?

What exactly wasn't this, Brody?

Your dick was hard because of him, stop denying it.

Okay, so my brain was a traitor.

Treason of the highest order, right along with my dick.

Fuck them both.

"You sure you're okay?" Miller asked, just as the elevator doors opened. Then he laughed. "Maybe the second bottle of champagne was a bad idea."

"Yeah, I mean, what could possibly go wrong?" I joked.

And then Carina spotted us, smiling at us holding hands. There was no cameraman this time, thank god.

"Are we ready for this?" she asked, far too excited.

"Always ready for food," I said.

"Did you get the champagne?" she asked.

"Uh, yes, he did," Miller replied.

I laughed. "You had some. It wasn't just me."

He leaned into my side, cute as hell, and gave Carina one of his charming smiles. "But yes, we are ready for food."

"Excellent! Come this way. Just a few formalities first," she said, leading us to what looked like conference room doors.

Again, my too-buzzed brain should have clicked a whole lot sooner . . . because she opened the doors and led us into a huge room full of people at tables. They stopped chatting, stared at us, and waited.

"Your attention, please," Carina said proudly. "Please welcome, Misters Miller Norton and Brody Molina."

Everyone applauded.

Oh, sweet mother of god.

Miller shot me a what-the-fuck look masked with a smile, and god knew what my face said. It must not have been good because Carina put her hand on my arm.

"Surprised?" she asked.

"Ah, yes," I squeaked. "Just a bit."

"Come in and mingle. There'll be a few photos before food is served."

She dragged us over to a group, who turned out to be execs from the contest organizer, plus the radio station sponsors, and other people I had no hope of remembering.

It was all such a blur.

We smiled, shook hands with everyone, posed for promo photos, and before too long, I was feeling far too sober.

Like he could read my mind, Miller plucked two flutes of champagne from a waiter. Smiling brightly, he handed me one. "What the actual fuck is happening?"

I downed half my glass and tried to smile back at him. "I have no idea."

"You didn't know this was happening?" His lips barely moved when he spoke.

"No clue."

"Did you read any of the terms and conditions before you entered us in this?"

My god. He could be a ventriloquist.

"It said it might include some promotional events."

"Jesus Christ."

"How can you speak without moving your lips?"

"Years of practice of asking what the fuck."

"You're good at it."

"Thanks." Then he laughed and shook his head. "One day we'll laugh about this."

"But today is not that day."

"No, it is not."

"Having a great time?" Carina asked, appearing from nowhere.

"Wonderful," Miller said, then he slid his arm around my waist and leaned into me. He felt like something warm and familiar, comfortable and safe. Like something I wanted to surround myself with . . .

It was so natural to put my arm around him and hold him to me. Sure, I'd touched him a million times, but this was far more intimate.

And I liked it.

And then his hand slid down to my ass and he pressed himself harder against me, his face almost in my neck.

His hand stilled on my ass, burning hot.

The only sane thing I could do in that moment was finish the rest of my drink.

"Aww, look at you two newlyweds," Carina said. "Hate to separate you, but I think dinner is being served."

I'd forgotten about food.

"Ah, perfect," Miller said, removing himself from me. "I'm starving."

I was starving for something else.

Him.

More of him curling into me like that. More of his hand wandering. More of his body heat.

This was insane.

Carina led us to our table, to our seats with our names on little placeholders, but before we could sit down, she called for everyone's attention again.

The room fell quiet, all attention on us.

Jesus Christ.

My mind was spinning.

While Carina spieled on about the promotion and

the sponsors, my brain was stuck on Miller. On this new fixation I had with him. This new attraction to him. To a man.

Not just any man.

To Miller.

The one solid thing in my life.

"Brody," Miller mumbled, his eyes telling me to pay attention.

I realized then that Carina had stopped talking, the room was waiting expectantly, the photographer was in front of our table, camera aimed and ready.

What the hell had I missed?

"They want us to kiss for a photo," Miller said.

"Kiss like newlyweds," someone hollered from the back.

"Kiss him like you mean it," someone else added.

People whooped and cheered, and lord almighty, this was embarrassing.

But Miller took my face in his hands and kissed me. Hard and open lips, our mouths melding for one long and perfect moment. My heart knocked so hard against my ribs that it hurt, and my everything felt electric.

But his mouth . . .

Warm, soft lips. No tongue.

I wanted his tongue.

I moved to deepen the kiss, just about to taste him, when someone cleared their throat.

Miller pulled back first, ducking his head, resting his forehead on my shoulder. "Sorry," he said.

What? He was sorry? I wasn't. I was only sorry I

didn't get to put my tongue in his mouth. But then he raised his head and looked right at Carina, not me. "Sorry," he said again. "Forgot where we were."

Oh. He wasn't talking to me.

People cheered, and as if that wasn't terrible and weird enough, we sat in our seats and food was put in front of us. Like I could stomach food right now.

I was dazed and confused, somewhat turned on, and embarrassed, and Miller was digging into his meal.

He stabbed some chicken and gave me a quick glance. "Chicken's good. You'll like it."

I looked at my plate. Right. Food. Yes, I should probably eat.

"You know," he added quietly as he ate, as if it were an errant thought, "I think we should practice kissing more. So you don't freeze up again."

My gaze shot to his. Well, to the side of his head. He wasn't looking at me. "I didn't freeze up. I zoned out. There's a difference."

He shrugged as he chewed another mouthful and swallowed. "Doesn't matter." He looked at me then, with a smirk, and he leaned in slowly so he could hide his mouth and whisper. "If you want to look bad, fine. This was your idea, so if it goes sideways, you're taking the rap for it."

Well, shit.

Could I practice kissing him?

Maybe it'd be good to get this new fascination out of my head. But mostly it'd be good training so I didn't try to give him tongue.

He stabbed a piece of chicken from my plate and put it to my lips. "Open wide," he murmured, voice low, eyes dark.

Was that . . . ?

Was he . . . ?

Was that sexual? Was he flirting with me?

Why was it so hot?

I opened my mouth like the desperate idiot I was and he slid the fork between my lips.

A few people laughed and I glanced over to see the closest tables watching us. Watching our every move, apparently. Like fucking weirdos.

Jesus H. Christ on a cracker.

"Fine," I mumbled to Miller. "We can practice."

He smiled as he chewed, pretending his meal was the most interesting part of this whole conversation. "How's your dinner?" he asked, blasé as hell.

"You mean my anticipation and regret salad? It pairs so nicely with my glass of what the actual fuck," I said, taking my said glass and downing it.

Miller laughed so loud that people looked at us. I mean, the people who weren't already watching us. But then he did that laugh and lean-into-me thing he hadn't done in months . . .

God, I'd missed him.

I'd missed our closeness and the touchy-feely way we used to be that, for some reason, in the last few months, he'd shied away from . . .

I put my drink down and put my arm around his shoulders instead, keeping him close.

"Anticipation and regret salad, huh?" he repeated as he stabbed some lettuce.

"Sorry," I tried.

"Oh, don't be. The regret's a given, but the anticipation is . . . unexpected." His eyes met mine then, and my heart damned near stopped.

"Unexpected," I squeaked stupidly, because he had no clue how unexpected this whole mess was.

Just then, a waiter appeared with a tray. "More champagne?"

"Yes, please," we both said at the same time.

"Keep them coming," Miller added. "We're gonna need them."

What was that supposed to mean?

"What was that supposed to mean?"

Miller put a glass of champagne in my hand. "To regret and anticipation," he said, raising one eyebrow at me. "And to a whole lotta what the actual fuck." Then he clinked our glasses and drank.

WE LASTED AS LONG AS WAS polite, then got the hell out of there and made our way through the anonymity of the slots and the crowds to the bar.

It'd been a busy day. Early start, the flight in, the stress of it all, two public appearances, a nap, and more alcohol than was probably wise.

"Two vodkas and soda," I said to the barman, throwing some cash on the bar.

"Was the champagne we drank today not enough?" Miller asked.

"No, it was not," I replied.

"So, is this drink to regret, anticipation, or what the fuck?"

The barman put two tumblers on the counter and I collected one, holding it up for Miller to cheers me. "I'm still going with all three."

He laughed and sipped his drink. I took a healthy swallow, clearly needing more courage than he did.

He put his free hand on my waist and leaned his hip against mine, his body fitting perfectly against me. It always had. We'd always slotted together so well . . . but now it was doing things to me.

I was suddenly hyperaware of his angles, his body heat, and how my hand felt on the swell of his ass.

How he leaned in to speak over the noise, how his stubble brushed mine, and for the first time in my entire fucking life, a jolt of pure electricity zinged through my whole body.

Stubble, for fuck's sake.

What the hell?

"Did you want to play?" Miller asked.

Yes.

Yes, I did.

. . .

Wait.

"Play what?"

He pulled back with a wicked smile and a spark in

his eyes. "The slots. Why? What did you think I was talking about?"

"Blackjack," I lied.

He laughed, his body still pressed against mine. I liked it in ways he was about to be able to feel.

"We can gamble tomorrow," he said. "I'm ready to head upstairs."

Oh boy.

"Yeah, same," I said, totally casual and cool. "I'm tired."

His eyes glittered when he chuckled, as if he knew I was full of shit but wouldn't call me out on it. He downed the rest of his drink, not moving away an inch, and I got a real close-up view of his lips on the glass and his throat when he swallowed.

Sweet mother of god.

My body was a tightwire, my head was a mess, and my heterosexuality was officially in fucking tatters.

I was going to go upstairs and make out with Miller.

I was going to kiss my best friend, and so help me, I was going to love it. It was going to change my life and everything I thought I knew about myself.

I was going to kiss him for real this time. As practice. And I could tell myself it wasn't real, but it was very fucking real for me.

"You ready?" he asked, looking at my not-empty glass.

I downed it quickly, swallowing the last trace of trepidation with it.

"As I'll ever be."

My stomach was a ball of knots as we got into the elevator. I was grateful other people rode it with us, and I avoided all eye contact in the mirrors. Mine, but mostly Miller's. He seemed to find something funny, and when we finally pushed through the door to our suite, he burst out laughing.

"Your face," he said. "Oh my god. Are you okay? You look like you're about to take a live landmine test. It's just kissing practice. We can do stage kissing if you want, so our lips don't even touch. Get the angles right, that kind of thing."

Before I lost my nerve, before he could back out, and before my heart stopped altogether, I strode over to him, took his face in my hands, and kissed him.

CHAPTER FIVE

MILLER

There was a look in Brody's eyes I'd never seen before. A jumbled mix of determination, pain, and desire.

I wasn't too surprised when he kissed me. We'd talked about it, after all. But I was surprised by the intensity.

I was surprised by how hot it was and how much he seemed to want it.

This was no practice kiss.

I was even more surprised when he slid his tongue into my mouth.

Hot, demanding, deep.

The jolt of desire, of the thrill, shot through every cell in my body. I tingled and melted and groaned like a porn star.

No shame. No turning back either, apparently.

It took me a full couple of seconds to kiss him back,

to pull him close, and when I fisted his hair, he grunted and broke the kiss.

We stood there, mouths open and panting, staring at each other, chests heaving.

I wanted to ask him what the fuck that was all about, but I didn't want to panic him. I didn't want this to end.

Brody could kiss like a demon.

His lips were swollen and red and wet, his pupils blown. I probably should have said or asked a hundred things, but only one word was on my mind.

"More," I mumbled, pulling him in for another kiss.

I led this time, my hands finding his hair. I tilted his head so I could deepen the kiss and taste every inch of his tongue. Our bodies pressed together, and I could feel his interest . . .

Holy shit.

He was getting hard.

This is happening.

This is actually happening.

I was kissing Brody, and he was kissing me right back.

I gripped his hair, then his jaw, his neck. Our tongues fought for dominance, tangling and sweet, and my whole body was singing. Every fiber in me wanted this, wanted him, wanted more.

Without meaning to, without thinking, I walked him backward to the wall. We hit with a thud and broke apart, kinda laughing . . .

Until reality caught up with him.

He put his hand up, meaning *stop*. His chest was heaving and he leaned forward to catch his breath, and after a few long seconds, his eyes met mine.

I was waiting for the freakout. For the anger and the outburst. But no. He smiled.

"Well, you sure can kiss," he panted.

"So can you," I replied, breathless. "You okay?"

He laughed again, but it sounded a little wilder this time. "Uh, undecided."

I didn't want him to panic. "Okay."

He shook his head and stood up to his full height, and when he looked at me again, he laughed. "So much for practice."

"I think we practiced pretty well."

He laughed again and ran his hand through his hair. "Pretty sure we don't need to kiss like that in front of anyone."

I shrugged. "Unless you wanna start an OnlyFans," I said. His gaze shot to mine and I laughed. "Just kidding."

He sighed and discretely tried to adjust his junk. He clearly thought it was as hot as I did.

For his sake, I pretended not to notice. "So, in the race of regret, anticipation, and what the fuck, which one's in front?"

He gently banged the back of his head on the wall a time or two. "Uh, what the fuck is definitely in the front."

I took his hand and led him to the sofa. "As long as

regret and awkward aren't in the running, we'll be fine."

He sat with a noticeable distance between us. "I wasn't aware awkward was even in the race."

I looked at the space between us. "It's not supposed to be."

He groaned. "Sorry."

"Don't apologize."

"I kissed you first, and—"

"And I kissed you back, so we're even."

He stayed silent for a bit, clearly trying to process.

"So," I hedged. "First time kissing a guy?"

"Yep."

"And?"

He balked and his cheeks flushed pink. "Uh . . . It was . . . fine."

"You said I could kiss."

He groaned and put his hands over his face. "Shut up, I was embarrassed."

"I'm going to use that against you forever now."

He tried to hit me with a cushion but I took it. "You said I could kiss too," he countered.

"And I meant it. I know now why Jessica Whitmore followed you around for a year. You kissed her, and that was it for her. Poor girl. I should message her and apologize." I put my hand to my chest. "Now that I know what you're capable of."

He glowered at me. "Not funny, Miller."

I snorted and tossed the cushion back at him. "Yeah, but now it's not awkward between us."

And that was the truth. I could make jokes and ease the tension. If I left it up to him, he'd be spiraling right now. Whereas I was used to shelving my emotions when it came to him. I'd been doing it most of my life.

He shook his head and licked his lips, and I wondered if he could taste our kiss.

"If you wanna talk about it . . ." I murmured.

"Can we not?" He looked at me then, and there was fear in his eyes before he looked away. "Sorry. Maybe later. Tomorrow."

"Okay." I didn't want to push. He was clearly trying to get his mind around what had happened and the fact that he'd been into it. "I'm gonna grab a quick shower." I stood up and headed for the bathroom. "Well, I dunno about quick. For as long as it takes me to jerk off."

A cushion hit the wall behind me, making me laugh.

I managed a quick shower, without the jerking off, and came out with the towel around my waist. Probably should have thought about grabbing my clothes before I'd gone in.

Brody was at the window, looking at the well-lit strip. His reflection in the glass was neon.

"Shower's free," I said.

He startled, turning around, then seeing me half naked, he groaned. "Christ, put some clothes on."

"You've seen me wear less than this. And tomorrow is the pool party. I'll be wearing *way* less than this."

He bit back a groan—one of frustration, I was sure —and dug his fingers into his eyes. "I'll . . . I'll go . . . shower."

He went around the couch to avoid me. "I didn't jerk off in there, if that helps."

He stopped at the door. "It . . . does not help, but thanks."

I snorted. "Brody," I began.

"Still don't wanna talk about it."

The door closed behind him and I changed into my PJs, which were a pair of gray sleep pants. It was all I ever wore to bed. But for his sake, I did pull on a T-shirt.

I turned on the TV and climbed into bed, pulling the covers up over my hips to save him from spiraling some more.

I probably shouldn't have joked with him about it. But damn, if I didn't make light of it, we'd probably fight and I'd say a whole lotta things I shouldn't, and we'd be taking separate flights home.

He took a while in the shower, doing what I tried not to imagine, and came out with a towel around his waist. "I, uh, I forgot my pajamas," he mumbled, quickly grabbing them from his bag and disappearing again.

Yep, he was definitely awkward. Normally he'd have pulled his briefs on under his towel, then flicked me with it.

But not now.

So maybe joking about it wasn't the best way to handle it . . .

He came back out, dressed in long boxers and a shirt—not his usual sleeping outfit either—and quietly got into bed.

"*Pawn Stars*," I said, waving the remote at the TV. "We should go there tomorrow and see if they're filming."

"Hm."

Awkward silence followed, and I didn't look at him, and the longer it went on, the more awkward it got.

I sighed. "If you don't want to kiss in public—"

"Still don't wanna talk about it."

Awesome.

Whatever.

"Fine." I tossed him the remote and turned onto my side, away from him. "Good night then. See you in the morning when we can pretend it never happened."

Exactly how I'd spent the last ten years of my life.

More silence, then the TV shut off, casting the room in darkness. Aaaaand more silence.

"I'm just trying to get my head around it," he blurted out. "I'm not having some gay-panic moment. I'm not, it's not that, it's just . . . It was my first time kissing a guy. And not just any guy, but you."

"Wow. Sorry to disappoint."

He growled in frustration. "I wasn't disappointed, for fuck's sake, Miller. I thought you'd be more understanding."

Well, that stopped me.

I rolled over to face him. "I can't be understanding when you won't talk to me, then you tell me the problem was not kissing a man but specifically because you were kissing me. Not sure how I'm supposed to take that."

"Because it wasn't a problem to kiss you," he said, clearly exasperated. "That's the problem."

"Okay, thanks for clearing things up."

"Jesus, Miller. Don't you get it?"

"Get what?"

"I liked it!" he cried, rubbing his hands over his face. "I liked it," he whispered this time.

Well, holy shit.

I reached out and took his hand. "It's okay, Brody. You're allowed to like it. And you're allowed to try new things and decide if it's for you or not. It's okay to maybe like it now and then decide no, it's not for you. There are no rules. So, no regrets, okay?"

He sighed and smiled, his eyes meeting mine in the dark. "Thank you."

God, how it made my heart flutter and ache at the same time.

"So, tomorrow," he hedged, wincing.

"Will you be okay with kissing or not? We can totally skip it if you want." Not that I wanted to skip it, but it felt like the right thing to say. "Kiss my cheek instead, or my temple. People love that. Or my neck . . . Okay, maybe don't kiss my neck, because that's my weak spot so that's probably not a good idea. Especially if I'm wearing Speedos."

He snorted out a laugh. "Oh god. Are you really?"

"Absolutely. It's a gay pool party, of course I am."

He groaned. "I'll be so out of my depth."

"Believe me, they'll love you. But stick with me and you'll be fine."

"Well, we're supposed to be husbands, so who else am I gonna be with?"

I snorted. "Oh, my sweet summer child. Tomorrow's going to be so much fun."

I WOKE up with Brody's arm around my waist, his nose in my hair, his dick pressed against my ass.

I'd dreamed of moments like this.

Specifically.

Oh so very specifically.

My whole body burned, my dick fully awake and ready, and it took physical effort on my behalf not to grind against him.

Oh god, how I wanted to.

And maybe if I did, he'd wake up and finish the job.

Or he'd wake up and freak out.

More than likely.

So I made a beeline for the bathroom and the shower had barely enough time to heat up before I was jerking off. I had to get rid of my boner before I wore a pair of tiny Speedos . . . before we pretended to be newlywed husbands who couldn't keep their hands off each other.

I got dressed and made coffee all while deliberately not looking at the sleeping Brody still in the bed.

Jesus Christ.

Enjoy it while it lasts, Miller. Because it all ends tomorrow when you fly back home to reality.

I heard the bathroom door close, and while he took *forever* in there, I decided tidying the suite a little was a good idea. And making him coffee and pretending everything was fantastically fine was too.

And apparently him not saying much at all was part of his plan.

Breakfast wasn't too awkward; we didn't need to pretend to be anything but two people eating breakfast together.

A few people smiled at us and said a cheery good morning to us, which was odd. Maybe they'd seen the promo stuff. Or maybe it was just a Vegas thing. The folks who were still drunk and hadn't slept yet were definitely a Vegas thing.

"Let's hit the strip," I suggested when we were done. "We have a few hours to kill."

Brody nodded. "Good idea."

So we wandered outside, into the disgusting heat and crowds. We avoided the hawkers and folks trying to shove flyers in our hands and made our way into Caesar's Palace where the AC was welcome. Then The Venetian, and fake Venice was kinda awesome. Then we visited the fountain, the Eiffel Tower, and Freemont. We laughed and took photos, took selfies, and it was habit to slip my arm into his as we walked back to our hotel.

We'd walked together like this, holding hands or arms linked, a thousand times over the years. But there was an uneasy feeling about it now.

It didn't feel like it used to.

I tried to pull my arm free, but he grabbed my hand instead. He looked away but his grip tightened, and I saw his throat as he swallowed. "I feel like tacos," he said.

Okay then.

So we had tacos.

It was after two by the time we made it back to the suite. "What time does this pool party start?"

"Three."

He groaned as he fell back onto the freshly made bed.

"I'd like to remind you that this whole weekend was your idea," I said, rifling through my suitcase for my pool party outfit. "So anything you are subject to doing against your will is completely your fault."

He whined. "I need sympathy, Mills."

When I looked over, he was in the fetal position. Dear god. I grabbed his ankle and dragged him to the end of the bed.

"Hey!" he said. "What the—"

"Get in here with me," I said, walking into the bathroom.

"What for?"

"Brody, I swear to god."

"Okay, okay," he mumbled, walking in.

I was standing in front of the mirror with my arm out. "Come here. We need to get our game faces on. We will be surrounded by gay men. Believe me, if there's one sniff of doubt about us being married, they will know."

"You make it sound like we're walking into a target range."

I snorted, because yeah . . .

I pulled him close, both of us facing the mirror but leaning into each other. "Put your chin on my shoulder," I prompted. "Hand on my waist, or my ass, whatever you're comfortable with."

He chose my waist.

"Relax," I said to his reflection. "We need to look comfortable."

He sighed and some of the tension left his body. "Like this?"

I nodded. "And when you touch me, mean it." I took his hand, stood in front of him so he was half behind me, and placed his palm flat on my stomach. "You want everyone there to know who you belong to."

His eyes met mine in the mirror. "Isn't that what the wedding ring is for?" He held up his left hand like it proved his point.

"They don't care about wedding rings, believe me. It's all about body language."

He made a face.

"Now. I'm going to touch you. Nothing lewd, don't worry," I added at the bewildered look on his face. "And probably nowhere I haven't touched you already. Arms, hands, waist."

"You make it sound like an undercover FBI operation."

I shrugged. "Well, what you said about target practice was kinda apt. If they get one sniff of available fresh meat, you're done for."

"Fresh meat?" He looked positively horrified. "Jesus Christ."

I gave him my brightest smile. "If you get overwhelmed or feel a bit out of your depth, just look at me. Stick with me and you'll be fine." Then, for good measure, I turned him around and smacked his ass. "Now, go get changed."

He wandered off like a lost child, and I couldn't help but smile.

He was so not ready for this.

CHAPTER SIX

BRODY

I WAS SO UNBELIEVABLY NOT READY FOR THIS.

Now, I'd been to gay bars before, mostly with Miller. I'd been hit on before while I stood at the bar and pretended not to watch him get it on with some random lucky asshole on the dance floor.

I had no problem being in queer spaces.

What I had a huge problem with was wearing nothing but swimwear with a near-naked Miller in a room full of testosterone and pheromones, with music pumping and Miller's hand on my ass. All while some barely dressed men stared at us while others were making out and grinding all over each other, and . . .

Yeah.

That's what my problem was.

I'd woken up with a raging hard-on, having dreamed all night of having Miller underneath me, naked and writhing, taking my cock over and over.

And, so help me god, rubbing one out in the shower this morning did little to help my situation.

Flashbacks of kissing him, how he'd taken my tongue, how he'd tasted, kept flashing through my mind. When he'd suggested we hit the strip, it'd been so much better than going back to our suite where I'd no doubt inevitably make things more awkward between us.

I didn't want it to be awkward.

I just wasn't sure how to deal with this.

How to deal with being suddenly attracted to my best friend.

How this could possibly ruin the best thing in my life.

And I thought he'd been exaggerating about the gay pool party . . . until we walked in.

Fashionably late, of course. We walked in and heads turned, whispers and nods in our direction . . . Hell, Miller wasn't exaggerating at all.

But one drink down and Miller had his shirt off, tucking it into the back of my shorts. I didn't even get to ask why because his shorts followed soon after, and he was happily parading around in a very small black Speedo.

His fine body, lean and muscular in all the right places, glinted like he'd moisturized . . . Christ, he'd moisturized.

A few men cheered and he responded by dancing, spinning in a circle, but quickly pulling me close.

My hand went to his lower back, fingers skimming the smooth fabric of his Speedo.

"You okay?" he asked, his lips near my ear.

"You weren't kidding about fresh meat," I mumbled.

He threw his head back and laughed.

We'd somehow made our way toward the pool, which had blow-up unicorns and beach balls and bronzed men on display. I was pretty sure one couple was having sex in the pool...

Oh god, they were, for real.

This was insane.

"Is it always like this?"

He shrugged and continued to dance. "This is Vegas, baby." Then he slid his hands to my hips and we danced.

Well, he danced with his arms up, and I tried really hard not to look down at his junk while he was facing me, or at his ass when he turned around.

He had a really great ass though.

"Oh," Miller said. "Sorry. Taken."

I stopped ogling his ass to notice a man in front of Miller, his hand on Miller's waist. Before I knew what I was even doing, I slid my arm around Miller and pulled him behind me and glared at the douchebag and his filthy hand. "He said he's taken," I growled.

The man put his hands up with a sly smirk and danced his way back into the crowd. Miller hummed in my ear. "Fuck, Brody, that was hot."

I was irrationally angry, stupidly protective, and now unsurprisingly more confused.

I met his gaze, surprised by the heat I saw in his eyes.

What I wanted to do was take his face in my hands and kiss him so he, and the other men, knew damn well who he belonged to.

But I couldn't.

So I put my fingers to his chin and lifted his face. "You belong to me."

Yep.

I said that.

Out loud.

To his face.

For fuck's sake.

And the funny thing about it? I meant every word.

"I always have," he whispered, eyes clear and as honest as I'd ever seen them. Then he took my hand. "God, I need a drink."

So we drank.

Bright-colored vodkas that were full of sugar and carbs that would probably kill me tomorrow, but right then, I'd have drunk anything.

Miller danced and laughed, his blue drink raised high as he swayed.

Men wanted him.

They eyed him from head to foot, and I saw them size up their chances until they saw me. He wasn't kidding when he said to keep my hand on him, and after a few orange and pink drinks, I danced with him so they'd know he was mine.

Which he wasn't. Not technically, but this weekend he was.

It helped that I glared at some of them until they backed the fuck up.

I was shirtless, my small black swim shorts riding high on my thighs as Miller danced against me.

I was going to have a raging hard-on at this rate, and my drunk ass couldn't bring himself to care.

If Miller got any closer, he'd definitely feel it.

I slid my hand to his hip and held him half an inch short of contact. What I wanted to do was hold his hips and grind hard against him, but at least I still had the sense not to.

He wiggled a little, testing my resolve.

"Probably not a good idea," I murmured behind his ear.

He turned his head. "What happens in Vegas . . ."

Christ.

That wasn't helping.

Drunk and flirty dirty-dancing Miller wasn't helping at all.

Because I didn't want this to stay in Vegas.

I wasn't sure I could.

How could I go back to our real lives and pretend none of this had happened? That I hadn't realized this about myself. That I was attracted to my best friend. That I wanted us to be more than friends.

Would I risk it all for a chance?

Do it, Brody. Do it now or you never will.

And I was drunk enough to think what the voice in my head said was a good idea.

What did he say before? Not to kiss his neck because it was his weak spot?

So what did I do?

I held his hips and as I brought his ass into contact with my dick, I kissed his neck. Open lips and sucking.

He froze for a split second before he arched his back, melting into me, then faster than I could stop him, he turned in my arms.

Well, we were certainly touching now.

From chest to thighs, his arms around my lower back, holding me in place. He could definitely feel my hard-on, and I could feel his interest growing. *God, it feels so good.* His eyes lasered in on mine, burning into me. "Brody," he murmured.

"I don't know what it means," I said, hoping no one else could hear. Hell, I didn't even know if he could hear me. I leaned in and whispered in his ear. "But I don't wanna fight it anymore."

He crushed his mouth to mine, kissing me deep, tongues tangling, and both our cocks jerked, sandwiched between us.

Yeah. I was done fighting this. Whatever it was. I was drunk enough to call this battle lost.

I didn't want to fight it. If I could have him in my arms like this, pressed tight against me with his tongue in my mouth, then yeah, I'd take the risk.

Miller's arms went around my neck as we kissed, right there in front of a few hundred strangers.

I didn't care. None of them mattered.

He mattered.

He was all that mattered.

I broke the kiss. "We need to leave," I said, breathless.

Before I embarrassed us in front of everyone. Even though I got the impression that this crowd wouldn't mind, I didn't want my first time doing anything with Miller to be in public.

"Yes, we do," he said, taking my hand and pulling me toward the door. We found the elevator, not even bothering to put shirts on, or even shorts, in Miller's case.

The elevator had people in it, which was probably a good thing. It took every ounce of self-control not to look down. To see if he was still sporting wood.

I didn't have to look at mine to know.

I kind of held my shirt in front of me so it wasn't obvious, which Miller found amusing.

"It's not funny," I whispered just as the doors opened on our floor.

We'd barely got inside our room before he pounced on me, taking my face in his hands and kissing me, pulling me so I pinned him against the wall.

Holy fuck, this felt so good.

Feeling how turned on he was just somehow made it better.

I pushed my hips hard against his and he lifted one leg, which I took, gripping his ass and grinding...

Slow down, Brody. Fuck, this'll be over far too soon.

I broke the kiss, trailing my mouth down his neck. "Should we talk about this?" I panted.

He craned his neck, giving me more room, and he fisted my hair. "Let me have this," he said, and I wasn't thinking clearly enough to follow. Then he jumped up, hooking his other leg around me so all I could feel was him. "Talk later."

Well, that I understood.

But now I had him pinned to the wall and his erection was rubbing against mine. I needed my hands to feel, to grip, to touch every inch of him, but I was holding him . . .

So I lifted him and carried him to the bed. He laughed as we hit the mattress, but he soon guided our mouths back together, grinding and rolling his hips slowly, dragging every ounce of pleasure out of each move.

I realized then, like a bucket of cold water, that I didn't know what to do next.

"I don't know what to do," I mumbled, still kissing him. "Teach me."

He groaned a sound so guttural it damn near lit a fuse inside me. And then he slid his hand between us, down my shorts, and gripped me.

Uh, yeah. There was no stopping now.

"Fuck," I bit out.

"Touch me," he whispered.

I did it without thinking, without getting lost in my head, that this was a man. Miller, no less. I simply pulled at his Speedo until I freed his erection, and . . . holy shit.

Could another guy's dick be pretty? Should it turn me on to see it? To hold it?

I wrapped my fingers around him and he arched his back, mouth open, and suddenly what he was doing to me wasn't anywhere near as important as what I was doing to him.

I technically had no experience in pleasuring another man, but I knew what I liked, so I went with that.

Long strokes, slow, with a twist over the slick head, over and over, and he was pulling me, squeezing the head of my cock, pumping the shaft, and then his fingers trailed down to my balls . . .

And I couldn't hold my orgasm back. I came, my cock spilling onto his stomach at the same time he arched with a cry, pulsed in my hand, his come mixing with mine.

Aftershocks ripped through me, intense and all-consuming, before I collapsed on top of him.

I didn't care that I'd just smeared our come between us.

In fact, I hoped I did.

I liked it.

Miller let his legs fall flat with a groan. He was panting, so sexy. "Damn."

"Is it always that hot?" I asked, my brain still too mushy to stop stupid words from spilling out. "Think I came in record time."

He laughed, rolling us onto our sides, but he was quick to keep hold of me, finishing with a sigh. "We'll need to shower."

"Dunno. I was just thinking how much I like the mix of our come on our skin."

He froze and pulled back. "Brody?"

"Welcome to the shocked and confused club," I said. "Membership's free."

His expression softened; his hand found the side of my face. "Confused and shocked, huh?"

"But not sorry." I blinked, slower than I'd have liked. "God. Orgasm and alcohol mean sleep. Talk later, 'kay?" I closed my eyes and pulled him in close, the smear between us squishing a little. I still didn't care. "As long as you're not going anywhere."

Did I say that out loud?

Pretty sure I did.

He snorted. "Well, I can't. considering we're now glued together."

"We're conjoined twins . . . come-joined twins."

He tried not to laugh. "Your pillow talk is terrible."

"Mm, funny," I said, too far gone to even open my eyes, let alone think. "Sleep."

I WOKE UP TO A DRY, crusty feeling on my stomach, and as if that wasn't gross enough when I opened my eyes, those pink and orange drinks came back to haunt me. "Ow."

"You shouldn't let jizz dry on your skin," Miller murmured. "It gets itchy and can cause skin irritations. First rule of sex with a man . . . Actually, it's probably not the *first* rule."

I rubbed my forehead. "No, my head hurts. What was in those cocktails?"

"Rocket fuel. Also known as the cheapest vodka on the market."

"Feels like it."

"You okay?" His eyes met mine for the briefest moment before he looked away. He wasn't asking if I was feeling okay. He was asking if I was okay with what had happened.

I sat up and took his hand, threading our fingers. "I don't regret it, if that's what you're asking. I have . . . concerns."

Now he looked offended. "About? If you're worried about my sexual health—"

I scoffed. "No. Not about that. I mean, we probably should discuss it at some point, but . . . my concern is about us."

He frowned at our hands. "What about us?"

"I don't want things to change between us. I mean, I do. I want everything to change, but not you and me. Does that make sense?"

"Not at all."

I sighed and winced and groaned, all at the same time. "My head hurts and I'm hungry. Should we order something? Pizza? I feel like pizza. Then we can talk."

He tried to smile. "Is it the 'it's not you, it's me' talk?

Because if it is, I think we can save ourselves the trouble and just skip it. Pretty sure I won't survive that. And I know this is all new for you, so if you'd rather just—"

"What? No, no. Can you let me talk?"

He took his hand away. "Sorry."

I snatched his hand right back. "Stop it. Look at me, Miller." I waited until his eyes met mine. "Yes, this is new to me. But you're not. There's no one on the planet who knows me like you do."

Right then, my stomach growled, and he laughed. "Pepperoni with peppers?"

I smiled at him. "See? You know me. And the way you pull my hair when you kiss me . . ." I shook my head slowly. "Damn. How did you know to do that to me?"

That earned me a smile. "I didn't."

"Well, it's a fucking thing."

He sighed and studied my eyes for a long moment, searching for the truth, no doubt. I hoped he'd see the sincerity.

"Miller, please. Don't shut me out. Let's talk about this. We can put everything on the table and see where we land. I don't know what it means, but I want to find out."

His lips twisted in a tormented smile. "I'll order us that pizza."

CHAPTER SEVEN

MILLER

He was saying everything right. Every single thing I'd ever wanted to hear, but it scared the hell out of me.

Because if this ended badly, I wasn't sure I'd survive it.

So while I felt like I was being handed the winning lotto numbers, this could cost me everything.

We got cleaned up and dressed and inhaled the first few slices of pizza in silence. It wasn't awkward, it was just both of us getting everything right in our heads first.

"So," he began, sitting back on the sofa, sipping his water. "I can think straight now, at least . . ." Then his gaze darted to mine and he winced. "Straight's probably not the right word to start off this conversation with."

I laughed and wiped my hands on a napkin, sitting back like he was. "Wow. You haven't made a straight joke since I came out to you."

"I didn't mean . . . I just . . . I'm trying to choose my words carefully."

I gave him a smile and a nudge. "Since when have you ever not said exactly what you're thinking? Just say whatever's on your mind, Brody."

"Well, you know. Labels are . . . weird. I don't know what it means or what this"—he gestured between us—"makes me."

"You don't have to use a label. Not everyone does. Some folks appreciate the understanding it gives them; some folks don't like the boxed-in feeling."

"I'm not gay."

"I know that. Your history of bedded women speaks for itself. All I'm saying is that if you liked what we did, then maybe—"

"I ain't bi, either."

Okaaaaay.

I put my hands up. "Okay. Fine. It's fine, Brody. You don't need to explain. I was just trying to help—"

"Shut up and listen to me. I'm trying to get this out." He winced again. "Sorry, sorry. It's just a lot, and I don't know what the fuck it means. I don't like men. I can see when a guy's hot, sure. But I have no desire to take him home. I have no desire whatsoever to initiate anything with a guy. I don't care how he looks at me or what he offers."

Okay . . .

"Have other men offered—"

He pulled at his hair. "Ugh, maybe, I don't even know.

They were never on my radar. But I like *you*. Not men. Not guys, not any other man on this planet. But you. I *desire* you," he said again, gesturing to me with both hands. "I don't know why. I can't explain it. But *you*. I see you, and I want to touch you, I want to kiss you, I want to do things to you. I want to push you up against a wall and feel you surrender to me. I want to do incredible things to you..."

Oh.

Oh, holy fucking shit.

He was saying the most amazing things. Everything I'd ever dreamed he'd say. But he looked so distraught and vulnerable, it hurt to see.

I closed the distance between us and took his hand. "Hey."

"I don't want to lose you, Miller. I don't want to ruin what we have," he said. "You're my best friend. You're the only person who knows me, who gets me. I can be myself around you. I can touch you and hold you, and maybe it'd be even better if I could kiss you whenever I want to. And other things, maybe. Definitely. But you. I want to be with you. I want to take you out on dates, cuddle on the couch watching your terrible TV shows. Your mom loves me, and my mom loves you more than she loves me. And that's fine. I get it. So yeah, I want things between us to change, but to stay the same, just get better."

I laughed and pulled him in for a tight, soul-fixing hug. "I've waited my whole life to hear you say that to me," I murmured. "God, Brody. My whole life, all I ever wanted was you. My straight best friend that I could never have."

He pulled back, his eyes on mine. "Your whole life what?"

I laughed. "Since the day we met, the only person I've ever loved is you."

His expression grew mildly concerned. "I was fourteen and had pimples and braces."

I snorted. "*We* were fourteen with pimples and braces."

His eyes searched mine. "You mean that?"

"Eleven years," I whispered. "I've pined over you, loving you from afar, brokenhearted every time you dated anyone new."

He frowned. "Oh, Miller. I'm sorry."

"Don't be."

"Is that what you meant when you said 'let me have this' when I asked if you wanted to slow down?"

I managed a nod. "Eleven years I'd dreamed of that."

He sighed sadly. "I had no idea."

"I know you didn't." I took a deep breath and steeled myself. I had to know. "Do you mean it now? Do you mean what you said about wanting me? Because I won't survive it if it's just a phase or a whim. My heart can't take another hurt from you."

He shook his head, his eyes wide. "I mean it. Miller, baby, I mean it. I was scared to tell you. I thought you might say no . . ." He frowned. "I noticed these last few months you'd been distant, and it scared me. That light in your eyes when you'd look at me was gone, and it scared the shit outta me. Maybe it made me realize that I'd taken you for granted all these years, and the thought of not having you made me look at what you truly are to me. That maybe I *did* need you to be more. That I wanted you in my life, that my heart needed you, wanted you, and maybe I'd been blind this whole time."

"Brody," I whispered.

"I couldn't lose you, Mills. And then I started to have feelings about losing you, and how much I missed being around you, and being able to touch you. And then I started to think *a lot* about touching you, and then it was *all* I could think about. Then it wasn't just touching . . ." He grimaced. "I'm sorry. That's a terrible thing to say. But I kept having inappropriate thoughts about what I wanted to do to you, and it was a first for me, lemme tell ya. I was weirded out, not gonna lie. Because it was you, my best friend. I shouldn't have been thinking of you like that. But it wouldn't go away. And then it wasn't weird anymore because it was hot." He shrugged. "And then I had the chance to bring you here. A weekend away. Just you and me. Where I could maybe make sense of my head, and where it wouldn't feel like you were leaving me."

I put my hand to his face. "I *was* leaving you, Brody," I admitted quietly. "I was trying to put some distance between us because I couldn't take it anymore. I was heartsore, and I hated myself for loving a guy who could never love me the way I needed him to."

"But I can," he said, his eyes full of hope. "I *do* love you, Miller. As my best friend, but more than just that.

You're my person and the person I want to be with. I don't care that you're a guy."

I laughed. "Uh, thanks?"

"I know I'm probably not explaining it right." He took a deep breath and pressed his forehead to mine. "I want to be with you, Miller. As your boyfriend, as your partner. Hell, I'll drive through the Elvis Chapel with you right now if that's what you want. I mean, we've been married all weekend and it's been kinda fun."

I snorted because he was joking. Surely.

He sighed, his eyes searching mine. "I love you, Miller. I want us to be together. I need you to believe me."

"I want to believe you," I whispered. "I've spent the last eleven years dreaming of this, so please understand why I have a hard time thinking this is real. Or that you could possibly know what it means to me."

"I know what it means," he whispered. "And I'll happily spend every day of forever proving it to you."

My heart was thumping so hard it hurt. So full, so happy.

Then he made a face, his cheeks pink. "Now, I know how to do a lot of things, but there are some things I'll need you to teach me." He winced. "Intimate things. I want to do them all," he quickly added. "God, I want to do everything. What we've done so far has been . . . well, hotter than hell. I mean, it's new and different, but holy fuck, Mills. I never knew it could be like this. And maybe it's because I have feelings for you. Because I do love you. Maybe that's why it's so intense with you. It's never been like this with anyone because I've never loved anyone the way I love you."

So maybe he was more demisexual than bi, but that was something for a later conversation.

I put my hand on his cheek and kissed him softly, my heart hammering that I could actually kiss him. "It's okay. I'll teach you."

He kissed me back, soft and warm. "Teach me how to love you," he murmured. "In every way, so you never want for anything, Miller. I want to be everything for you."

I closed my eyes. "You already are." I slid my hand down his back and pulled our hips together and kissed him, deeper this time. I let his tongue invade my mouth, and we fell back onto the sofa, him on top of me, between my legs, my arms tight around him. It wasn't hurried; it wasn't the heated passion from earlier. This was a recognition of everything we'd just said.

He was showing me his sincerity.

He certainly wasn't weirded out by being with a guy, and he was pressing against me in all the right places. I slowed the kiss to a stop. "So," I said, looking into his eyes. "Those things you want me to teach you, the things you imagined doing to me . . ." I couldn't help but smile. "Wanna tell me what they were?"

He chuckled, embarrassed, ducking his head into my neck. "Hm, I seem to remember you saying you loved your neck kissed." So, of course he sucked and kissed my neck, sending shivers of pleasure through me.

I gripped his hair and pulled the strands, making him groan as his mouth found mine again. Things were starting to heat up when he pulled back, a pained expression on his face. "I didn't bring any condoms."

I scoffed. "Whoa. Moving pretty fast there. Is that what you dream about?"

His face burned red, but his eyes scanned mine. "Well, yeah. I want to do that. I keep thinking about what it would be like to sink into you and—"

"Oh my god," I blurted. But my dick twitched, and my balls drew down.

"Is that . . . is that not what you . . . ? Oh god, I'm sorry, I—"

I laughed and pulled him in for a kiss. "It's fine. Just unexpected. And fast. For what it's worth, yes, I want that. I want that very much, but maybe we could work up to that?"

His grin was sheepish. "Oh, of course. Sure. Good idea."

He began to pull back off me so I grabbed him, pulling him right back. "I never said we were done. We have all night. Unless you wanna head downstairs to the casino. We haven't tried our luck at anything."

He grunted, kissing me hard before he whispered, "I already won the jackpot, Mills. I have a lot to learn and a lot of time to make up. If you're gonna teach me, I wanna start tonight."

My laughter died in my throat when he rolled his hips.

I gave him two lessons that night. Frottage, which he clearly loved, and me sucking his glorious cock. Which he also loved.

The rest of the pizza went cold, and Vegas partied long into the night without us.

I HAD NO REGRETS, and from the way Brody couldn't stop grinning at lunch—because we'd slept right through breakfast—I could assume neither did he.

Or when we were in the lobby checking out, he took his phone and FaceTimed his mom. "Hey," he said, not caring that the lobby was full of people.

"Oh hi, love," she replied, her smiling face filling the screen. "Your dad's right here. Where's Miller?"

He turned the phone to show me, but then he pulled me in close, kissing me right in front of her before he grinned at her again. "Mom, we have some news!"

Okay then.

He was not being shy. He really was serious about this . . .

She squealed, then nudged his dad. "You owe me twenty bucks."

Brody stopped smiling. "Huh?"

His dad's face filled the screen. "Goddammit, Brody. You cost me twenty bucks."

He blinked. "Uh, I'm sorry, what?"

"Your mom bet me twenty bucks that you and Miller would . . . well, you know, one day you'd pull your head out of your ass and realize that boy loves you—"

"Oh my god," Brody said.

"Oh my god," I said, embarrassed, stunned. "Thank you, Mr. Molina."

Brody looked at me. "They had a bet on me."

I snorted.

Mrs. Molina's face reappeared. "You can tell me all about it when you get back."

Well, not *all* about it.

Mr. Molina leaned in. "Don't forget, Brody, next weekend you said you'd help me prune the trees in the backyard. Bring your boyfriend, two for the price of one. Easiest twenty bucks I ever spent."

"Oh my god," Brody said again.

"He doesn't mean it," his mom said. Then she waved. "I'm happy for you boys, finally! Okay, I can see you're busy. Let me know when you get back, and we'll see you both soon!" Then her hand appeared. "Now, how do I turn this off . . . ?"

Brody hit the End button. "They could have acted surprised," he grumbled.

I laughed. "They took it well."

"They had a bet on me!"

Then Carina appeared like a genie in a puff of smoke. There was no photographer this time, thankfully. "How was your weekend? I trust you had a good time."

I looked at Brody and he smiled at me. "Best weekend ever," he said.

God, the way he looked at me made my heart thump. "The best."

"We, uh, we didn't see much of Vegas though, sorry," Brody said, grimacing, blushing.

She laughed, guessing all too well why we didn't get out much. "Just so you know, follow your hashtag on our social media page. Lots of pics from the pool party yesterday."

Oh great.

"Awesome," I said, trying to smile. "I think?"

She laughed. "Oh, believe me, you'll love them." Then she looked at us both. "So how will you settle into married life when you get back? It's all so new, right?"

Newer than she realized.

"Slowly," I replied.

"But surely," Brody added, sliding his hand into my back pocket and squeezing my ass.

"Off to the airport now?" she asked.

"Yes, we kinda slept in, so we should go. Don't wanna miss our flight." I shook her hand. "Thank you for everything. It's been . . . amazing."

"It sure has," Brody agreed. "Life-changing, even."

We said our goodbyes and made it to the airport just in time to board the plane. We fell into our seats, and Brody was soon scrolling through his phone.

He'd found the photos from the pool party that Carina had mentioned, and he saved a lot of them.

Pics of us dancing, of us kissing, of him with his hands on me.

They were hot, not gonna lie.

Then he began loading the photos into a post on his Instagram.

"What are you doing?" I asked.

"Gonna get this over with right now," he said. "Saves telling everyone separately, right? Also helps that my phone is about to be in Airplane Mode for an hour, so . . ."

I chuckled. "If you're ready, then sure."

His eyes met mine. "I am." He hit Post, and the comments began rolling in.

Finally.

OMG finally.

About fucking time, Brody.

Yes! Looking hot, guys . . . also about time, Brody, you dumbass.

He made a face at his phone. "Your sister just called me a dumbass." Then he looked at me. "Have I been that oblivious?"

I laughed. "Uh, maybe."

My phone beeped with message after message, but I didn't even look.

We turned our phones off and he took my hand, thumbing the ring on my wedding finger. Then he looked at his own fake wedding ring. "Not sure I wanna take mine off," he murmured. "I know it's not real, but maybe we could wear them on our right hands until we decide to do it for real."

My gaze cut to his. "Brody."

"I told you I mean it. I've never been surer. Everyone in our lives seems to have known this but me. I feel like an idiot. And I feel even worse for stringing you along for so long."

Oh, damn.

Then his whole face brightened. "We can come back here, anytime you want, and get hitched by Elvis."

"Do you think our mothers would ever let us do that?"

"Probably not. But it's Vegas, so . . ."

I took the ring off my left hand and slipped it onto his right hand, then took his off his left and put it on my right. "When we're ready, we'll do it for real. Without Elvis."

He grinned. "Deal." He spent a few long seconds looking at my ring on his finger.

"Regret, anticipation, or what the fuck?" I asked.

His eyes met mine. "Regret I didn't realize sooner, anticipation for what's next, and *what the fuck* did you do with your tongue last night because it's all I can think about."

I laughed, still not believing that any of this was real. "You know, when we were on the plane coming here, I remember thinking this whole weekend would have its own chapter in the book of the stupidest shit I'd ever done."

He stared at me and blinked. "And now?"

"The stupidest," I said with a smile. "And without a doubt, the best."

He leaned over and kissed me. "The very best."

"You know, we never even placed a bet all weekend."

"Nope. Mighta helped if we'd got out of bed occasionally," he said. Then he lifted my hand and kissed my knuckles. "I still won the jackpot though."

I laughed. *He's so cheesy and ridiculously sweet.*

But I'd been losing this game for eleven years, and now, after rolling the dice one last time, I'd finally won. I still couldn't believe it was real. I met his gaze and saw nothing but love looking back at me. "Dunno. Pretty sure that jackpot's mine."

~The End

ABOUT THE AUTHOR

N.R. Walker is an Australian author, who loves her genre of gay romance. She loves writing and spends far too much time doing it, but wouldn't have it any other way.

She is many things: a mother, a wife, a sister, a writer. She has pretty, pretty boys who live in her head, who don't let her sleep at night unless she gives them life with words.

She likes it when they do dirty, dirty things… but likes it even more when they fall in love. She used to think having people in her head talking to her was weird, until one day she happened across other writers who told her it was normal.

She's been writing ever since…

---

nrwalker.net

ALSO BY N.R. WALKER

Blind Faith

Through These Eyes (Blind Faith #2)

Blindside: Mark's Story (Blind Faith #3)

Ten in the Bin

Gay Sex Club Stories 1

Gay Sex Club Stories 2

Gay Sex Club Stories 3

Point of No Return – Turning Point #1

Breaking Point – Turning Point #2

Starting Point – Turning Point #3

Element of Retrofit – Thomas Elkin Series #1

Clarity of Lines – Thomas Elkin Series #2

Sense of Place – Thomas Elkin Series #3

Taxes and TARDIS

Three's Company

Red Dirt Heart

Red Dirt Heart 2

Red Dirt Heart 3

Red Dirt Heart 4

Red Dirt Christmas

Cronin's Key

Cronin's Key II

Cronin's Key III

Cronin's Key IV - Kennard's Story

Exchange of Hearts

The Spencer Cohen Series, Book One

The Spencer Cohen Series, Book Two

The Spencer Cohen Series, Book Three

The Spencer Cohen Series, Yanni's Story

Blood & Milk

The Weight Of It All

A Very Henry Christmas (The Weight of It All 1.5)

Perfect Catch

Switched

Imago

Imagines

Imagoes

Red Dirt Heart Imago

On Davis Row

Finders Keepers

Evolved

Galaxies and Oceans

Private Charter

Nova Praetorian

A Soldier's Wish

Upside Down

The Hate You Drink

Sir

Tallowwood

Reindeer Games

The Dichotomy of Angels

Throwing Hearts

Pieces of You - Missing Pieces #1

Pieces of Me - Missing Pieces #2

Pieces of Us - Missing Pieces #3

Lacuna

Tic-Tac-Mistletoe

Bossy

Code Red

Dearest Milton James

Dearest Malachi Keogh

Christmas Wish List

Code Blue

Davo

The Kite

Learning Curve

Merry Christmas Cupid

To the Moon and Back

Second Chance at First Love

Outrun the Rain

Into the Tempest

Touch the Lightning

EWB - Enemies With Benefits

Holiday Heart Strings

Bloom

The Men from Echo Creek

Method Acting

The Bait

TITLES IN AUDIO:

Cronin's Key

Cronin's Key II

Cronin's Key III

Red Dirt Heart

Red Dirt Heart 2

Red Dirt Heart 3

Red Dirt Heart 4

The Weight Of It All

Switched

Point of No Return

Breaking Point

Starting Point

Spencer Cohen Book One

Spencer Cohen Book Two

Spencer Cohen Book Three

Yanni's Story

On Davis Row

Evolved

Elements of Retrofit

Clarity of Lines

Sense of Place

Blind Faith

Through These Eyes

Blindside

Finders Keepers

Galaxies and Oceans

Nova Praetorian

Upside Down

Sir

Tallowwood

Imago

Throwing Hearts

Sixty Five Hours

Taxes and TARDIS

The Dichotomy of Angels

The Hate You Drink

Pieces of You

Pieces of Me

Pieces of Us

Tic-Tac-Mistletoe

Lacuna

Bossy

Code Red

Learning to Feel

Dearest Milton James

Dearest Malachi Keogh

Three's Company

Christmas Wish List

Code Blue

Davo

The Kite

Learning Curve

Merry Christmas Cupid

To the Moon and Back

Second Chance at First Love

Outrun the Rain

Into the Tempest

Touch the Lightning

EWB

Holiday Heart Strings

Bloom

The Men from Echo Creek

Method Acting

SERIES COLLECTIONS:

Red Dirt Heart Series

Turning Point Series

Thomas Elkin Series

Spencer Cohen Series

Imago Series

Blind Faith Series

Missing Pieces Series

The Storm Boys Series

Gay Sex Club Stories

FREE READS:

Sixty Five Hours

Learning to Feel

His Grandfather's Watch (And The Story of Billy and Hale)

The Twelfth of Never (Blind Faith 3.5)

Twelve Days of Christmas (Sixty Five Hours Christmas)

Best of Both Worlds

TRANSLATED TITLES:

ITALIAN

Fiducia Cieca (Blind Faith)

Attraverso Questi Occhi (Through These Eyes)

Preso alla Sprovvista (Blindside)

Il giorno del Mai (Blind Faith 3.5)

Cuore di Terra Rossa Serie (Red Dirt Heart Series)

Natale di terra rossa (Red dirt Christmas)

Intervento di Retrofit (Elements of Retrofit)

A Chiare Linee (Clarity of Lines)

Senso D'appartenenza (Sense of Place)

Spencer Cohen Serie (including Yanni's Story)

Punto di non Ritorno (Point of No Return)

Punto di Rottura (Breaking Point)

Punto di Partenza (Starting Point)

Imago (Imago)

Imagines

Il desiderio di un soldato (A Soldier's Wish)

Scambiato (Switched)

Tallowwood

The Hate You Drink

Ho trovato te (Finders Keepers)

Cuori d'argilla (Throwing Hearts)

Galassie e Oceani (Galaxies and Oceans)

Il peso di tut (The Weight of it All)

Pieces of You - Missing Pieces 1

Pieces of You - Missing Pieces 2

Pieces of You - Missing Pieces 3

Code Red

FRENCH

Confiance Aveugle (Blind Faith)

A travers ces yeux: Confiance Aveugle 2 (Through These Eyes)

Aveugle: Confiance Aveugle 3 (Blindside)

À Jamais (Blind Faith 3.5)

Cronin's Key Series

Au Coeur de Sutton Station (Red Dirt Heart)

Partir ou rester (Red Dirt Heart 2)

Faire Face (Red Dirt Heart 3)

Trouver sa Place (Red Dirt Heart 4)

Le Poids de Sentiments (The Weight of It All)

Un Noël à la sauce Henry (A Very Henry Christmas)

Une vie à Refaire (Switched)

Evolution (Evolved)

Galaxies & Océans

Qui Trouve, Garde (Finders Keepers)

Sens Dessus Dessous (Upside Down)

La Haine au Fond du Verre (The hate You Drink)

Tallowwood

Spencer Cohen Series

Thomas Elkin One

Lacuna

GERMAN

Flammende Erde (Red Dirt Heart)

Lodernde Erde (Red Dirt Heart 2)

Sengende Erde (Red Dirt Heart 3)

Ungezähmte Erde (Red Dirt Heart 4)

Vier Pfoten und ein bisschen Zufall (Finders Keepers)

Ein Kleines bisschen Versuchung (The Weight of It All)

Ein Kleines Bisschen Fur Immer (A Very Henry Christmas)

Weil Leibe uns immer Bliebt (Switched)

Drei Herzen eine Leibe (Three's Company)

Über uns die Sterne, zwischen uns die Liebe (Galaxies and Oceans)

Unnahbares Herz (Blind Faith 1)

Sehendes Herz (Blind Faith 2)

Hoffnungsvolles Herz (Blind Faith 3)

Verträumtes Herz (Blind Faith 3.5)

Thomas Elkin: Verlangen in neuem Design

Thomas Elkin: Leidenschaft in klaren

Thomas Elkin: Vertrauen in bester Lage

Traummann töpfern leicht gemacht (Throwing Hearts)

Sir

So Unendlich Viel Liebe (To the Moon and Back)

THAI

Sixty Five Hours (Thai translation)

Finders Keepers (Thai translation)

SPANISH

Sesenta y Cinco Horas (Sixty Five Hours)
Los Doce Días de Navidad
Código Rojo (Code Red)
Código Azul (Code Blue)
Queridísimo Milton James
Queridísimo Malachi Keogh
El Peso de Todo (The Weight of it All)
Tres Muérdagos en Raya: Serie Navidad en Hartbridge
Lista De Deseos Navideños: Serie Navidad en Hartbridge
Feliz Navidad Cupido: Serie Navidad en Hartbridge
Spencer Cohen Libro Uno
Spencer Cohen Libro Dos
Spencer Cohen Libro Tres
Davo
Hasta la Luna y de Vuelta
Venciendo A La Lluvia
En la Tempestad
El Toque del Rayo
Corazón De Tierra Roja
Corazón De Tierra Roja 2
Corazón De Tierra Roja 3

Corazón De Tierra Roja 4

ECB (Enemigos con Beneficios)

Floral

CHINESE

Blind Faith

Bossy

JAPANESE

Bossy

To The Moon and Back

PORTUGUESE

Sessenta e Cinco Horas

www.ingramcontent.com/pod-product-compliance
Lightning Source LLC
LaVergne TN
LVHW040156080526
838202LV00042B/3191